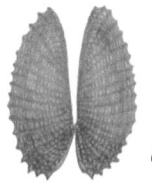

Who says an angel can paint?

Miranda Jones would never make such a claim.
Her skill has begun to put her in the limelight and her artistry is being admired both in San Francisco, where she grew up, and in Milford-Haven, where she moved a few months ago.

But being an artist is hard work as far as she's concerned, and she takes it seriously. Rather than waiting for inspiration—or for a so-called angel's touch—she buckles down, researches her subjects, perfects her technique, and turns out work she's grateful to be able to complete.

She chooses her subjects . . . except when they choose her.
Having decided upon a "hand-made Christmas" this year, she has thoughtfully planned each gift, from the hand-carved box for her friend Samantha, to the hand-sewn placemats and napkins for her artist's rep Zelda, to the original presents for her parents and sister. It all made sense . . . until a strangely irresistible impulse had her painting the image of a rugged cliff with a ragged rope hanging across its face. Why? Who is it for?

Milford-Haven is particularly delightful during the holidays.
Decorative lights twinkle along Main Street, adding cheer and special appeal to the quaint array of shops and cafes. Delightful aromas waft from store to store as shop owners outdo one another offering baked goods and spiced drinks.

Miranda feels more cheerful during her first Christmas in her new town than she has in years. Yet even in the midst of her holiday preparations, she feels so driven to commit this ominous image to canvas, it's almost as though it's being painted by a hand other than her own.

Why did she feel compelled to complete the odd little painting so urgently? Since it doesn't feel appropriate to display it in the gallery, who will ever see it?

Come discover for yourself . . . ***When Angels Paint.***

THE PRESS PRAISES
THE MILFORD-HAVEN NOVEL SERIES

In Mara Purl's books the writing is crisp and clean, the dialogue realistic, the scenes well described. I salute her ingenuity."

– Bob Johnson, Former Managing Editor, *The Associated Press*

"Every reader who enjoys book series about small town life has a treat to antici-pate in . . . Mara Purl's Milford-Haven Novels."

– Dee Ann Ray, *The Clinton Daily News*

"Mara Purl's characters have become old friends and I keep expecting one of them to give me a call!"   **– Nanci Cone,** *Ventura Breeze*

". . . an intrigu[ing] cast of diverse characters."

– Fred Klein, *Santa Barbara News Press*

"You can't escape the pull of Milford-Haven, the setting for *Days of Our Lives* actress and award-winning author Mara Purl's enticing new novel *What the Heart Knows.* My kind of romance, this [is a] juicy, read . . . plus, the inviting story makes you think."   **– Charlotte Hill,** *Boomer Brief*

"I read Mara Purl's *What the Heart Knows* and loved the book—just devoured it, in fact—and can't wait to read the next installment."

– Anne L. Holmes, APR
National Association of Baby Boomer Women

ENDORSEMENTS FROM OTHER AUTHORS

"Mara Purl is a skillful storyteller who has written a charming and tantalizing saga about the ways in which lives can intersect and be forever changed. The first novel in the saga is not-to-be missed."   **– Margaret Coel**
New York Times **Best-Selling author of the** *Wind River* **series**

"I found a kinship with . . . your heart for character . . . and with your truly fine unveiling of story events."   **– Jane Kirkpatrick, Author**
Wrangler Award, Willa Award

"I so admire Mara Purl's writing style. The pictures she paints are just glorious, her characters and attention to detail inspiring."   **– Sheri Anderson**
Emmy Award-winning writer, *Days of Our Lives*
Author, Salem Secrets Series

When Angels Paint

Mara Purl

When Angels Paint

A Milford-Haven
Holiday Novelette

Bellekeep Books

When Angels Paint ©2011 & 2019
Painting Angels ©2005
Milford-Haven
PUBLISHING, RECORDING & BROADCASTING HISTORY
This book is based upon the original radio drama Milford-Haven ©1987
by Mara Purl, Library of Congress numbers SR188828, SR190790, SR194010;
and upon the original radio drama Milford-Haven, U.S.A.
©1992 by Mara Purl, Library of Congress number SR232-483, broadcast
by the British Broadcasting Company's BBC Radio 5 Network, and which
is also currently in release in audio formats as Milford-Haven, U.S.A.
©1992 by Mara Purl. Portions of this material may also appear on the
Milford-Haven Web Site, www.MilfordHaven.com or on
www.MaraPurl.com © by Mara Purl. All rights reserved.
An earlier version of this story was published as
"Angel on a Rope" in the "Christmas Angels" collection ©2005.

For information address: Bellekeep Books
29 Fifth Avenue, Suite 7A, New York, NY 10003
www.BellekeepBooks.com
Front Cover – Original Watercolor by Mary Helsaple ©2018
Front Cover design by Reya Patton & Nick Zelinger
©2018 by Milford-Haven Enterprises, LLC.
Copy Editors: Vicki Werkley & Derra Moyers
Interior Design: Rebecca Finkel
Author photo: Ashlee Bratton

Published in the United States of America
E-Book Creation 2019

CIP pending
ISBN: 978-1-936878-52-9-29

For Caren Pearson
and For Mary Helsaple,
who make the world more beautiful
by painting.

Acknowledgments

Thanks to my publishers: Patrice Samara, Kara Johnson and Tara Goff at Bellekeep. Thanks to my gifted editorial team: Vicki Hessel Werkley, editor; Jean Laidig, second editor, proofreader and layout designer. Thanks to Mary Helsaple for exquisite cover art, to Tara Goff for cover design, and to Nick Zelinger and Rebecca Finkel for superb graphics.

Thanks to my marketing team: Jonatha King and King Communications for PR and marketing; Kelly Johnson for Internet and social media wizardry; Sky Esser and Amber Ludwig for web design. And thanks to Judith Briles, Amy Collins, Joan Stewart and Kathy Meis for marketing wisdom.

Thanks to those who provide expertise during my research: for "Miranda," to artists Mary Helsaple and Caren Pearson for inspiration and depth of detail; for "Cornelius," to Dr. Laurence Doyle for off-the-charts, inspired brainstorming and astronomical specifics. Thanks to dear friends in the Central Coast who've supported Milford-Haven for many years with such enthusiasm, including Elaine Travel Evans, Kathe Tanner, Susan & Brent Berry, Judy Salamacha, Carol Schmidt and Dennis Eamon Young.

Thanks for support from fellow members of WWW (Women Writing the West), CLAS (California Literary Arts Society), IBPA (Independent Book Publishing Association), The Authors Guild, and Author You—serving with worthy colleagues on boards and advisory boards teaches me so much.

And most important of all—thanks to you, my readers! I'm thrilled to welcome those of you who are new to my books. And I extend a special heartfelt thanks to my ever-expanding core group of readers however we connect: at book clubs, book events, writers' conferences, teaching sessions, through my newsletter and via social media. I cherish each of you.

The Radio Drama

Milford Haven had its first air date in 1907, and my thanks go to KOTR in Cambria, California, our first radio home. In its next incarnation, Milford-Haven, U.S.A. was broadcast on the BBC, for which I thank Ms. Pat Ewing, Director of Radio 5—a maverick network that launched a maverick show and celebrated with us when we reached 4.5 million listeners.

In the U.S., thanks to New York's Museum of TV & Radio and Chicago's Museum of Broadcast Communications, for honoring the show by adding it to their permanent collections. And to Bill Bragg at YesterdayUSA.com, who first broadcast the show on internet radio. Thanks to Jim Kampshauer at KTEA in Cambria for the marvelous revival broadcast of the series.

Before there were any shows to air, there were talented actors, and my thanks go to both the original cast of Milford-Haven and to the cast of Milford-Haven, U.S.A., seasoned professionals who brought my characters so vividly to life that their work is inextricably woven into the fabric of the characters themselves.

Before there were actors to record, there had to be a studio, and my thanks to Engineer Bill Berkuta, whose Afterhours Recording Company became our studio home—a workshop in which we created one hundred episodes of the first show, sixty of the second, scores of Student Theater & Radio (S.T.A.R.) productions, and now audio books.

Thanks to Marilyn Harris and Mark Wolfram, who composed the haunting Milford-Haven theme and all the music cues that supported the emotional ebb and flow of the story, and whose music we now use for the Milford-Haven Novels Audio Books.

And before there was a Milford-Haven, there was a young woman who had always lived in cities—Tokyo, New York, Los Angeles. I spent a summer performing Sea Marks at Jim and Olga Buckley's Pewter Plough Playhouse in Cambria, and became fascinated with life in and of a small town.

Thanks to my U.S. listeners, especially those in Cambria and the Central Coast. Thanks to my U.K. listeners, particularly those in Milford Haven, Wales. Both these special towns have embraced me as an honorary citizen.

Thanks to my family and friends—supportive from day one: my late parents Ray & Marshie Purl; Linda Purl, Erin Gray, Caren Pearson, with very special thanks to Miranda Kenrick, and to Vickie Zoellner. My love and thanks to my husband Larry Norfleet.

And finally, thanks to my characters, among whom are: Jack, Zack, Miranda, Zelda, Samantha, Sally, Kevin, Joseph, Cornelius, Meredith, Shelley, June, Chris, Burt, Delmar, Emily, Wilhelm, Stacey, James, Mary, Russell, Nicole, Susan, and Cynthia . . . who are building, buying, painting, conniving, planning, dishing, cogitating, dominating, observing, consulting, beach-combing, serving, sleuthing, skulking, detecting, reporting, abusing, enduring, nurturing, scheduling, ordering, showing, sneaking and seducing, respectively.

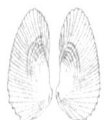

Dear Reader –

Welcome to Milford-Haven! For your inaugural holiday season visit, it's my pleasure to introduce you to my favorite little town and to a few of its many residents—all of whom are described in the Cast of Characters for the series near the end of the book.

This novelette features artist Miranda Jones, and gives you a glimpse of her new life in a small coastal town. The story stands alone as a complete tale, but also is woven into the overall tapestry of the Milford-Haven saga. Chronologically, *When Angels Paint* is concurrent with the holiday story *Where An Angel's On a Rope,* both of which conclude on the Eve of Christmas Eve—December 23rd. You'll find previews of that company story at the end of this little book. And you'll also find other previews in the series.

Miranda grew up in a wealthy Bay Area family where Christmas meant elegant shopping sprees and sumptuous gifts. Determined to make her first holiday season in Milford-Haven a "homemade" one, she finds first an unusual series of synchronicities, then an eerie sense that guides her to paint a most unexpected subject, leaving her with a heightened sense of the magic of the season.

Now, I invite you to settle in for a cozy holiday read that reveals Miranda's special delight is enjoying her very first Christmas season in her new home town.

As this story unfolds, follow my footsteps over the interconnected pathways of those who inhabit Milford-Haven, and come to that magical time of year when angels do unusual things . . . perhaps they'll even paint.

Mara Purl

"The universe is full of magical things patiently waiting for our wits to grow sharper."

— Eden Phillpotts

"Painting is the most magical of mediums."

— Chuck Close

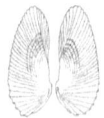

Prologue

With a paintbrush dripping red, dawn splashed color across tall coastal pines, creating a picture postcard.

Milford-Haven nestled against the rugged coastline while roseate light played across hillsides and shimmered in the chilly Pacific.

It was the perfect way for December twenty-second to begin. With three short days remaining till Christmas, the town would soon bustle with last minute purchases and long planned gatherings.

Eateries offered special additions to their menus. At Sally's, patrons ordered eggnog muffins and eggs sprinkled with nutmeg and parsley. At the Bird's Nest, cinnamon sticks swirled into hot apple cider and the eggs benedict came with slices of honey-baked ham.

Lives intertwined like strings of holiday lights, unfurled now to brighten Main Street and heighten the magic of the season.

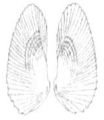

Chapter 1

Miranda Jones sat on her living room couch, blanket tucked around her legs, kitty curled in her lap, sipping her first cup of tea, watching as first light teased at her clerestory windows. With the beauties and comforts of home surrounding her, she tried to figure out the source of her unease.

First, there was a vague ambivalence about Zack Calvin that hovered at the edge of her mind like a fog bank standing just offshore. They'd been seeing each other—sort of. They'd enjoyed special times last week. Today was Monday, and just last Friday, he'd invited her to attend a Doobie Brothers concert at the Central Coast Bowl then invited her backstage afterward. Four days earlier, while she'd been down in Southern California, he'd gotten her a pass to watch the band rehearse at the Hollywood Bowl show in Los Angeles.

Since he'd been one of the concert organizers, he'd been very busy, and she understood why he hadn't had much time for her during, or after, the shows. He *had* suggested she come to Santa Barbara during the holidays, which she'd declined because of her own family obligations.

Her *head* told her all these reasons why they had yet to spend any real time together made sense. Yet her *heart* murmured something else—something about conflicting currents that she couldn't explain, but felt as an occasional undertow.

Perhaps they really would have a relationship one day, and this was part of its slow development. She sighed. *I'll think about him later. For now, I have so much to do!*

And that irritated her too. By today she'd expected to have nothing left on her list but to wash out her brushes and make a trip to the Enchanted Forest to cut some pine boughs for her mantle. Now she'd given up on that excursion, and was beginning to wonder if she'd make her self-imposed deadline.

Her plan had been to make it a handmade Christmas this year, her first in her new home town. She'd started by making her normally well-ordered painter's studio into a Santa's workshop. But still on her to-do list remained one more small painting, a box of silvered pine cones to which she must yet affix ribbons, and three tablecloth-and-napkin sets still to be stitched.

She'd done so well at first! Her original greeting cards were finished in October, and she mailed them immediately after Thanksgiving. She'd painted herself a new set of Christmas mugs and had them fired at the local kiln. The pine cones were painted before Halloween, and the lengths of ribbon long since set aside to be drawn through the tiny metal eyes drilled and glued into the end of each cone. She'd even done a small painting for Zack, a gift she'd mailed, even though she was still so unsure of her feelings. And she'd completed miniatures for close friends.

But somehow she'd been lulled into a false sense of security by her early endeavors, and in the usual Christmas rush, her professional art deadlines pressed her personal craft projects off the calendar. She'd managed to get some of them completed, wrapped, and shipped. But those that remained unfinished and unwrapped, she'd have to mail today, meaning they'd be late, arriving after Christmas. *So mad at myself! I'll just have to hope that late gifts will extend the holidays. Frustrating, when I actually got started so early. That, and the emotional uncertainty of—no, she thought. I'm not thinking of him any more today.*

Easing her legs out from under the still-sleeping Shadow, she drew a hand across the lush black fur, and couldn't help but smile when her pet uttered an annoyed "Meh," as if to insist she wouldn't be denied the last, best hour of sleep. "You put me in a better mood, kitty, even when you're in a bad one yourself."

Miranda walked the few steps to her kitchen—glad she wore warm socks—then took a swig of orange juice, a bite of cold bran muffin while she reheated water for a second cup of tea. After drizzling honey into her mug, she poured boiling water over a strainer of strong, black Darjeeling.

As gold rays spilled through her kitchen window and hit the small tree she'd decorated, Miranda sipped the hot tea and tried to summon again the Christmas spirit that'd inspired her crafts projects.

As light glinted off the shiny new sea horse ornament she'd found at Shell Shock—the beautiful shell store on Main Street owned by her friend Shelly Larrup—Miranda couldn't help but smile. *Maybe that's where it all started—memories of our childhood ornaments and shopping with Mother at Gump's.*

The famous San Francisco store presided over the its regional retail hierarchy like the reigning queen, and never was she more elegant than at Christmas. With Miranda and her sister in tow as little girls in red dresses, their mother would swirl through the store, climbing the wide wooden staircases to floor after floor. As little legs grew tired, Mother marched onward, bribing them the promise of hot cocoa at nearby Ghiradelli's after shopping. But fatigue vanished when her little princesses arrived at the stuffed animal department, where all three of them would clap their hands gleefully at Mr. Bear riding by on his choo-choo train.

Mother had started the tradition of giving each daughter Gumps signature blown-glass ornaments, one per year for each of them. Whimsical and colorful, they shone like spun-sugar gems on the family tree each year. Miranda remembered some of her favorites—the Santa riding a sea horse that'd inspired her recent purchase at the local shell store. But many others including the mustachioed Nutcracker, the White Rabbit, and the startled Gingerbread Cookie.

As adults, Miranda and her sister had taken up the tradition themselves, presenting their mother with a growing collection of eggs to rival those of Faberg'e in style, if not in price. Their first was Gump's Egg Nativity—the holy family housed in a miniature oval diorama. In following years, they'd given the Floral Champagne, the garden-themed and the elaborate turquoise. Meredith had picked out the ballerina one year, tiny pink tool skirt floating over delicate toe-shoed feet.

Now all the Gump's collections remained safely in their storage boxes until her parents decorated for the holidays. This year, perhaps they'd stay hidden away, as the family would all be traveling to New York.

Taking another sip of tea, and feeling somewhat bouyed by the pleasurable memories of childhood shopping, Miranda recalled she'd been determined this year to find a better way to celebrate than the usual compulsive round of buying.

That had sparked an argument with her parents, when they'd first broached the subject of a trip to New York.

"The Manhattan stores, all decorated for the holidays, Miranda!" Mother had trilled. "They're so gorgeous, and we haven't seen them in years!"

"But it's my first Christmas in Milford-Haven. Besides, I don't need anything," Miranda had complained.

"Nonsense. Every woman needs something at Christmas. And you've done your penance in that soup kitchen."

In previous years, while still living in San Francisco, Miranda had volunteered every year—though her mother had threatened to disown her for squandering her time and energy.

Maybe my crafts projects idea was me pushing back against the store-bought traditions. Whatever her reasons, this year she wanted to do something unique. It was not just her hands, but her talent she wanted to put in service. Having challenged herself to discover some way of serving others with her artistic abilities, she'd come up with the "handmade Christmas" notion.

So this year, she didn't allow herself to purchase any completed gifts, but conceded only the buying of raw materials. Then, as her projects got under way, she found a childlike pleasure in creating surprise gifts for others. She reminded herself of this as she glanced at her watch and sighed. *Not only do I have to finish my gifts, I also promised to take a shift at the gallery later.*

Fortified with the tea, she stepped into painting clogs and looked around the studio. Like patients in an over-crowded waiting room her half-finished projects seemed to stare at her accusingly. *Time for triage,* she murmured to herself. The completed demi-sized pieces were now dry enough to wrap, so they could be discharged. But the pre-cut table linens needed stitches.

She'd planned to create three tablecloths with matching placemats and napkins for her sister, her mother, and Zelda. She'd made a practice set for herself first. The seams hadn't been quite straight, but she'd been content to make mistakes on her own linens, hoping she'd have perfected her technique before sewing the gifts.

She'd chosen the fabrics carefully to suit each woman's personality and decor. Knowing she wouldn't be visiting her business representative in person, she managed to complete and mail Zelda's set in advance. The fabrics for the remaining two sets were already cut; she had only to hem them. And these sets she could deliver in person when she joined her family. So, this being one of the easiest tasks, she decided she'd feel better if one project were completed immediately.

Opening her sewing box, she found bright Christmas red for Meredith and special gold thread for her mother. Working on her sister's first, she placed the red spool on her sewing machine and began to wind a bobbin. But as the machine accelerated it only spun the bobbin across the room, where the tiny plastic wheel disappeared under a shelf.

Exasperated, Miranda got to her hands and knees to search for it and was reaching a long arm into unknown territories of dust and spiders, when a pin-prick stuck her finger. Jerking her hand back, she flattened herself to peer under the shelf and was greeted by gleaming gold eyes. Shadow—obviously in full delight—made a little chortling sound in her throat, eager to begin a grand game of fetch.

Chuckling herself, in spite of her annoyance, Miranda edged a hand toward her cat and tweaked her whiskers. Shadow leapt backward, hit the leg of a dining chair, startled herself into a one-eighty midair spin, then dove after the plastic bobbin, shooting it across the room.

Miranda rolled onto her back and laughed out loud before collecting herself to rise and retrieve the bobbin from her enthusiastic kitty. Realizing she'd have to negotiate for it, she looked for something to offer in trade. Nothing intrigued her cat more than the crinkling, bright gleam of a tiny ball of foil. Tearing off a piece from the aluminum roll, Miranda scrunched it and watched as Shadow responded to the enticing sound.

Tossing the new toy across the large room, Miranda watched as it skittered on the hardwood floor, Shadow in desperate pursuit. With her cat otherwise engaged, Miranda scooped up the hijacked bobbin and returned to her sewing tasks. Straight seams slipped handily along the guidelines of the old Singer. By the time another hour had passed, all the stitching was completed, and Miranda tied the bow on the last of the linen gifts: a spectacular frosted gold ribbon circled the dull sheen of silver satin paper, and under it Miranda slipped a hand-lettered note in a lovely cursive:

for Mother
Love, Miranda

After carrying the two wrapped packages downstairs to add to her luggage, she climbed back to the kitchen, made herself a third cup of tea and looked around the room. Despite two hours of work, it seemed she hadn't made a dent. And then the phone rang.

"Hello?" she answered, trying to keep irritation out of her voice.

"Well, dear, they're perfect."

"Zelda?"

"I don't know how you managed."

"I'm so glad you—"

"It's quite uncanny. I've looked everywhere for this bur-gundy color! It's precisely what I wanted for the table. I already had the candles, you see, and the dining chair slipcovers I had made in London years ago."

"Good, it did seem—"

"I'm beginning to think there is a Santa, after all." Miranda laughed.

"Oh, and the borders—they're the same pattern as the fleur-de-lis imprint on the napkin rings."

"What?"

"You must have had them made to order, clever girl."

"Well, I did make them, but I didn't—"

"Oh! My sauce! Sorry to run, dear, but I'm cooking. Merry Merry! Ta ta."

With a decisive click, Miranda's business manager hung up her end of the phone, leaving Miranda chuckling and pleased with herself. *I did do something right after all, she thought. Not a moment too soon.*

Though her house was in order her studio was chaos. Thank goodness she'd mostly finished packing, because tomorrow she'd be flying to San Francisco, then joining her parents and sister on a red-eye flight from SFO to JFK. *We'll arrive Christmas Eve morning. And I'm still not quite ready!*

Focus, she thought. She could tie the bows onto the cones later, when she'd exhausted her mental capacities and was zoning out in front of the television, probably watching the four-hundred-fiftieth rerun of Frank Capra's *It's a Wonderful Life.* She had to run her errands later—a few gifts to deliver and a stop at the post office. Tomorrow would be busy, too: brunch for her friends, then a long shift at Finders Gallery.

Today, that left completing the last of her 5x8 paintings. Sighing, she realized that unless she did it now, she'd never do it at all. The finished ones rested on small easels she'd wrap together with the paintings. Though she could have mass-produced several that were alike—Christmas trees or red doors with wreaths—she'd decided, instead, to create original pieces for each of the special people in her life.

She loved the one she'd done for her friend Sally O'Mally. The home-cooking in Sally's Restaurant had long since made it the heart of Milford-Haven, and the small town had come to depend upon her fresh ingredients and reliable recipes. The first painting for Sally was an interpretation of the restaurant in season—Christmas cake on its counter, windows bordered with holiday lights, on each table a tiny Christmas tree, and Santa sitting at the counter. It seemed to capture the mood of the cheery place perfectly, and she hoped Sally would enjoy it year after year.

Coming up with something for Kevin had been easy. He was almost as enamored of wildlife as she herself, particularly of the small creatures who came to visit his house from the adjacent forest. So for him she'd painted an opossum clinging to a tree, wearing a tiny Santa hat.

For her dear friend Samantha, the image that had come to her was the Pier jutting out from the Santa Carlita Cove. In the small image, the pier itself held Christmas delights—from a carousel to a tiny tram for tots—and the railings were outlined in multi-colored lights. The finishing touch was a little girl being held by her father, leaning as far as she could over the edge of the pier to accept a gift from a sea otter: a seastar—the perfect tree-topper.

For all her close friends, she now felt satisfied she'd captured just the right images. Yet somehow, the painting projects still seemed incomplete. She'd bought enough small canvases to create eight images, and only seven were filled. *Who is this last one for?* She wracked her brain again, trying to summon a name, but no one came to mind. Yet she'd learned to trust her intuition when a painting was trying to come through. *This must be for an unknown friend . . . maybe someone I don't even know yet.*

Now she faced again the blank canvas. Small though it was, it still seemed to overwhelm her painterly abilities, and she stood frustrated in front of her easel. Stuck, stuck, stuck, she complained. *Maybe music would help.*

Walking to her player, already loaded with Christmas CDs, she pressed the "Random" button and listened as strains of Celtic harp filled the room.

Suddenly inspired to wrap gifts while she listened, she reached first for the present she'd painted for her Welsh friend. Helen, a fellow artist, lived in the other Milford Haven—the one in Wales. With the press of time, usually they exchanged nothing more than e-mails, but for Christmas Miranda had painted her an elaborate Celtic cross. *She'll be lucky to get this in time for New Years, but I think she'll still enjoy it.*

As Miranda finished tying a bright green bow, the music shifted to a traditional carol played in an Appalachian style. *Music for every gift,* she thought, reaching for the one she'd created for her Aunt Madelon in Virginia—a painting of a dulcimer, with red ribbons secured under the tuning pegs. She tied the package with the same colored ribbons she'd painted to echo the gift inside, and knew the detail wouldn't escape her aunt's notice.

Reaching again for a present to wrap, Miranda picked up the piece she'd done for Kuyama, the Chumash Elder who'd bought two of her pieces. In honor of Winter Solstice, Miranda had painted a ceremonial pipe. From it, where a feather would normally hang, she'd added, instead, a gold leaf of tobacco, a plume from its smoke circling upward through the image.

As she finished the package with hemp paper and a raffia tie, she heard the strains of Indian flute. Carlos Nakai, she noted. But what struck her was that, again, the music seemed to match the particular gift she was wrapping. *Synchronicity*, she thought.

It seemed to be the theme today. What had Zelda said? That the burgundy table linens had been exactly what she was looking for? Certainly the thought encouraged Miranda. But it seemed odd in a way—to have hit the nail so firmly on the head. She almost never chose anything Zelda liked—their tastes were so different. Perhaps she was just being polite. If so, even that was a rarity. *Must be the Christmas spirit.*

The haunting flute music drew her back toward her studio, and she reached for her palette and paintbrush. Now it wasn't words, but images that filled her mind. As though a storm were gathering over her easel, dark grays and pale tans flowed through the end of her brush and swirled onto the canvas.

Unaware that her entire collection of Christmas music was playing through, Miranda continued to work. When the CD player clicked off, the small sound acted like the snapping fingers of a hypnotist, and she came out of her trance. Standing back, she surveyed the unexpected image on her canvas. Now from behind menacing clouds, a shape emerged—a sheer rock face below a mountain silhouette.

What is this? she asked herself. *And where?* Though she hiked the nearby mountains regularly, this didn't look familiar. Neither the image—nor her drive to paint it—seemed to make any sense. Yet it filled her with foreboding, and she shuddered in response. Where the piece was taking her, she still couldn't tell. But from long years of experience, she knew better than to doubt her intuitive process.

Time seemed to tug at her sleeve, and she glanced at her

watch. It was now nearly twelve-thirty p.m.. She wad meeting Samantha for lunch in an hour, and before business hours ended, she had to complete her errands. *Still don't know why I painted this . . . or who it's for. Doesn't seem to have anything to do with Christmas . Well, I'll just leave it here to dry.*

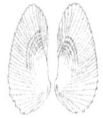

Chapter 2

Placing the already addressed gift bags in her duffel, Miranda struggled out the front door. Shadow darted past her, scampering into the front yard. "Okay, Girl," Miranda said. "You can stay out for a while."

Glancing across the street, she noticed the CCT logo on a truck. Central Coast Trees serviced the pines in her neighborhood once a week. *Working during Christmas week, she noted. Guess they'll be here on New Year's Eve too.*

Hefting the bag into her Mustang, she headed down the hill to the post office, where she found a line snaking out the door. *Why did I wait till the last minute?* she chided herself again, parking at the far end of the street. But as she took her place in the queue, she found herself joining in the Christmas camaraderie of her fellow townspeople.

A good-natured, rotund man was holding forth with Santa jokes when Kevin emerged from the building. "Hey, Miranda!"

"Kevin!" she said. "This saves me a trip!"

"Oh." Her tall friend brightened. "Me too. I grabbed your package. Need me to run an errand for you, or something?"

"You did? I mean, that's great," she said. "Now, I need you to stand right there, close your eyes and put out your hands."

"Oh, boy!" he cried, as expectant as a child. "I'll hold your box in one hand, it's small enough."

"Okay," she said, taking the five-inch square box he held and placing his gift on his outstretched hands. "You can open."

By now the strangers in line were enjoying the moment as well. Kevin ripped into the wrapping paper. "Wow, thanks!" he said, grinning at the opossum in the Santa hat. "I *have* one of those!"

Laughter erupted from everyone standing close enough to see the image.

"No, really! He lives in the pine at the edge of my property —only without the hat."

After bending down to give Miranda a big thank-you hug, and a promise to see her the next day, Kevin left. Half an hour later Miranda was relieved her packages were safely en route to their destinations. *Better late than not at all, she thought. Hope their delayed arrival will bring some after-Christmas magic*

She climbed into her car, then glanced at the return address on the little box. "It's from Mother," she said out loud, surprised, since she'd be joining her parents soon. She set the package on the passenger seat and started the engine.

Her next stop was Sally's Restaurant, and Miranda looked forward to another Santa's errand. She pulled open the screen door. It squealed, as always, then banged shut behind her. Sally O'Mally looked up from behind the counter she was wiping. But there was no accusation on her face—only a happy smile and a bright "Merry Christmas!"

"And to you," said Miranda.

"I'm real excited about tomorrow. I'll bring the eggs, and all the spices I'll need," Sally promised. "It'll just be me, though. Tony's doin' some big project."

"Great. You're both playing Santa. Nice earrings."

Touching the little bells that hung from red strings, Sally smiled. "Well," she drawled with her Southern twang, "Tony's favorite Christmas song is 'Jingle Bell Rock,' so I figured these was the ones to wear."

"Perfect," Miranda agreed. "Got a minute?"

"Sure. Ain't too busy at the moment, and we're gonna close early."

With a smile, Miranda handed her the red plaid package, she added, "This is for you."

"For me?" Her eyes widening, her fingers felt the outline of the gift inside the wrapping. "What is it?"

"Open it and find out," Miranda replied.

Shaking the package, Sally gave her friend an expectant look and carefully lifted the edges of the paper. "Oh, don't tell me," she said. Then, looking at the painting, she gasped, "Well *forever more!*"

Miranda laughed, enjoying every moment of her friend's delight.

"It's ... it's ... it's my very own place, all done up and all," she babbled. "It's the strangest thing—you got all the decorations I put up, but you got the ones I jest only *thought* of too!"

Sally gave her friend a fierce hug, then disappeared into the kitchen, to reappear a moment later with a hammer and a nail. Reaching as high as her arms would allow, she drove the nail into the wall next to her cash register. Then, retrieving her painting, she hung it. "And that's where it's gonna stay *every year!*" she exclaimed proudly. "I just love it!" Sally pressed the edge of her apron to her eyes, gave her friend another hug, and made a dash for her kitchen.

Still smiling, Miranda seated herself at her favorite table, just in time for Samantha Hugo's arrival. Miranda and her tall, red-haired friend ordered bowls of tomato basil soup and some home-made biscuits, then placed gifts for each other on the table, eager to open them before their food was ready.

"Gorgeous package," Samantha said. Lifting it, she asked, "A book?"

"Maybe," Miranda replied, keeping the mystery as long as possible.

"Hate to rip this," Sam said. Placing the gift on the table, she used her nails to peel tape from the bottom of the package, then pressed the green foil paper open. She gasped. "This is spectacular!" In the center of the wrapping lay a journal composed of a smooth, tan leather cover that wrapped around a blank book —just the size and style Sam always used, though hers were never this elegant. "Thank you! It's so very special."

"You can slide a new blank book inside when this one is filled," explained Miranda.

"Exactly!" Sam shook her head. "What a lovely way to start the new year." But it was as Sam turned the book over that she gasped again. "Oh!"

The front cover of the journal was fashioned as a frame, into which Miranda had slid the small painting she'd done for Sam. Gazing at the image for a long moment, Sam looked up at her friend quizzically. "Did I *tell* you my idea?"

"What idea?"

"About the Pier?"

Miranda thought for a moment. "No, I don't think so."

"I figured I must have because now you've painted it."

"What do you mean?"

Samantha gave her friend a piercing look, then said, "Maybe you're going psychic on me. I've been thinking about a project. My idea is to use the Pier to put on a special Christmas event each year. It'll be something fun for the children to do, and a fundraiser for toxic clean-up at the same time."

"That sounds wonderful!"

Inspecting the image carefully, Sam continued, "What's so strange is . . . well, this is just how I saw it. Bright lights on the Pier..."

"Rides for the kids?" Miranda asked.

"A cotton candy machine. . . ."

"Don't tell me you imagined the starfish?"

"No, you got me there."

As they laughed, their food arrived, and they cleared away the gifts, then sank their teeth into Sally's fresh, hot biscuits.

"Pretty intuitive, Miranda," said Sam between spoonfuls of soup.

"I guess we got the same e-mail from the Universe." When their late lunch was finished, Miranda opened her gift from Sam—a rosewood box carved with a mountain scene, its interior designed to hold watercolor supplies.

Stunned for a moment, Miranda was silent.

"Do you like it?" Sam asked anxiously.

"I *love* it," Miranda said. "It's just that . . . how did you know?"

"Well, you said you wanted to go to Colorado next fall, to do autumn watercolors."

"Well, the thing is," Miranda explained, "I just did a painting something like this."

Sam frowned. "Hmm. I found this one in Santa Barbara. The storm over the mountain—it has such elemental force. Made me think of you."

"Wow," Miranda said. "Thank you so much, Sam."

They stood to go and Miranda waved goodbye to Sally, then joined Sam in the parking lot. "Still don't know how you knew," Sam reflected as she unlocked her car.

"Ditto!" said Miranda, hugging her friend. "See you tomorrow!"

As she drove home, Miranda was full of Christmas cheer and gratitude for another year of friendships. But there was something more. It seemed to her the list of coincidences had grown very long today. As her car began the climb through the pines, she wondered if, unwittingly, she'd bitten off more than she bargained for. She'd wanted to be of service this year. *Did my simple request tune me in to a higher set of frequencies, the most obvious symptom of which was the synchronicity I've been experiencing all day?*

There was no answer to her rhetorical question, and she carried the small box from her mother inside, walking in her front door tired, but eager to finish packing. Glancing around, however, seeing what a disaster-area she'd made of her living room, she knew she'd have to clean things up first.

Fabric scraps were put back in her large sewing box, along with bobbins and spools of thread, her sewing scissors and pin cushion. Next she gathered the sheets and scraps of wrapping paper, all of which fit neatly inside the trunk she'd painted and now used as her living room coffee table. She enjoyed the economic use of space and considered it both a practicality and a pleasant secret.

It was as she was winding the last of the holiday ribbons that she came across the lengths of heavy green silk cord she planned to tie around some of her decorative pillows. As she pulled the silk rope from its package, it slid through her hands and she felt inexplicably drawn back to the easel in her studio. It seemed a matter of some urgency to leave the final clean-up and add to the painting of the clouds and rock face.

Standing in front of the image, she found her earlier foreboding shift to an encompassing dread. Unable to separate her emotional reaction from her creativity, she paced her studio, examining the painting from every angle. Getting a glimmer at last, she thought, *Something's missing.*

Picking up her brush, she breathed deeply and asked for guidance from the source she thought of sometimes as Love, sometimes as Mind. A moment later she found herself outlining a rope that seemed to hang down from nowhere and disappear off the edge of the escarpment. When she'd completed the details of the rope with its twists and frays, she again stood back to examine the piece.

Most of it was sheer rock face offering few places a person might find a foothold or a grip. It looked a daunting place, and yet the rope seemed to provide reassurance. *Like a promise,* she thought. The painting now gave her a sense of satisfaction. But beyond that, the picture still made no particular sense. Trusting she'd understand it at some later date, she returned to cleaning up the rest of her wrappings.

An hour later, standing to stretch, Miranda glanced out her windows, surprised to see only a faint rim of red lingering at the horizon. *Gets dark so early this time of year.* She checked the time—a couple of minutes before 5:00—and recalled that Shadow was still outside. Opening the front door, she called to the kitty for a couple of minutes.

Then, seeming to pop out of nowhere, the lithe animal darted inside. *No wonder I named her Shadow!* Like a shape-shifter, the unpredictable creature seemed to have turned from wild panther to domestic pet, and now pranced into the kitchen to circle her bowl.

"I know, you're just as hungry as I am," Miranda said.

"Meooooww," Shadow agreed.

"Let's see what we can do about that."

At the sound of the can opener, the cat seemed to drool, then purr as her dinner arrived. Shadow was too busy eating to notice the sound of a second can being opened—this one some Hearty Vegetable Soup, which Miranda served when it was heated, alongside a toasted mini baguette. Settling herself at the dining table, she flipped on the television, managing to catch the last hour of *The Ghosts of Christmas Past,* a special starring Ossie Davis.

After washing her dishes, she began readying her home for tomorrow's brunch. Over the few months Miranda had lived in her new town, she'd been gradually creating a set of dishes for herself. Though she didn't fancy herself a potter, she'd part-nered with a local expert who knew how to give plates enough uniformity to stack and match nicely. It was painting the glazing that intrigued Miranda, so, after perfecting a design in her own studio, she'd tried her hand with the potter's help.

Now, she was the proud owner of six place settings: bread, salad, and dinner plates, soup bowl and mug. She'd chosen coastal pines as her theme, which were perfect for, but not limited to, the holidays. Her tree pattern marched around the circumference of the sturdy-looking mugs, and stood together as small forests in the center of the various plates. To avoid having the soft white background look like snow, she'd added a pale wash of blue at the upper edges of her repeating image, then filled in some tan brush strokes on which the trunks rested. Finally, at the heart of each plate-picture, she'd added the outline of a small house. When she signed the back of each piece, she title the series "Home."

To carry out her theme, she'd found fabric that matched quite well for the runner, placemats and napkins she'd sewn for herself. She stretched the runner down the table's center, now, and added the miniature Christmas trees she'd found in a craft store. Soon the linens, candlesticks, dishes and flatware made a festive display of her open dining area, and she grinned at the prospect of sharing it all for the first time tomorrow.

At last, table set, kitchen ready, living room spotless, Miranda glanced around once more, spotting the small box from her mother. *Wonder what it could be?*

She doubted it'd be a gift, since they'd be sharing Christmas. In which case, it must be something needed for her here at home. She carried it downstairs to change into her pajamas. Her suitcase, which lay open on the floor, beckoned, but she knew she'd have time to pack properly tomorrow.

Using a metal nail file, she slit open the packing tape to find the contents bubble-wrapped. *Something breakable?* Mystified, she found a note folded inside, carefully written in her mother's hand on her cream-colored stationery.

> *Miranda dear,*
> *I know we'll all be together soon, but I also know you're starting new traditions in your new town by the ocean. I thought your little hummingbird painting was most charming. So, thought you'd enjoy the enclosed for your first Milford-Haven Christmas tree.*
> *Love, Mother*

Miranda sat on the edge of her bed, stunned for a long moment, Then, her curiosity piqued, she began peeling the bubble wrap. The squeaky crackle brought Shadow bounding up onto the comforter.

"What do you think, Kitty? What can it be?"

Shadow opened her mouth as if to answer, but only emitted a small chirrup.

As Miranda turned over the last fold of plastic, a satin-smooth arc of glass lay gracefully across her palm, long beak at rest, small wings pulled back as though ready for flight, and one bright eye staring upward. She gasped, the vision of the tiny bird such a perfect match to one last summer, the live one she'd held in that same hand until it'd flown away.

A small, printed card read, "Gump's Red Hummingbird Christmas Ornament." The artist had captured perfectly the S-curve of the small body, choosing solid red for the back and on the white front the bejeweled appearance of tiny rubies. On its head, worn like a crown, sat the golden circle by which the ornament could be hung from its slender red ribbon.

"I never even knew Gump's made a hummer. How could she have known, Kitty?"

Shadow offered no reply, though her attention did seem rapt on the small avian visitor.

"Oh, Mom." Miranda felt her throat constrict and her eyes begin to fill. "You could've knocked me over with a feather." She choked out a laugh. "Well, in fact, you did!"

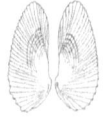

Chapter 3

When she'd come downstairs, Miranda'd been looking forward to a good night's sleep. Now she found herself pondering again the sense of synchronicity that'd punctuated her day like words echoing in the chorus of a song.

Samantha's gift to her. Her own gift to Sally. Now this ornament from Gump's, when Miranda'd been practically fixated on the family's collection.

As she brushed her hair before bed, Miranda looked into the mirror, her own troubled expression confronting her. Tired though she felt, a sense of unease tugged at the edges of her mind. *A gift I left out?* She tried to remember. *Something still to do before I leave tomorrow?* As far as she could recall, everything was finished.

Still uneasy, she trudged up her stairs one more time and switched on the kitchen lights to check what she'd written on a pad of newsprint she used as her running to-do list. Her finger traced down the column of reminders hand-written in green ink. No omissions. Yet the sense of something being wrong persisted.

Pay attention, she told herself. *Intuition's never wrong.* Time and again she'd proven this to herself. She'd get a feeling about returning a phone call, accepting a job or taking a different path while hiking. But those were actionable, sixth-sense directions that were protective or practical. This was different because it was vague.

Caught in an unsettled, nervous energy, she flipped off the kitchen lights, turned a table lamp on to its lowest setting and plopped onto her sofa to gaze out the window, where the last traces of light had long since faded and the early dark of winter had overtaken the landscape. A field of stars sparkled against a black satin sky—but the view was blocked intermittently by the dark silhouettes of tree trunks. *Like my insights today, blocked by things I can't really see.*

Something pulled her attention back into the room, and her eyes swept across a bookshelf. The thick, black spine of an over-sized volume was adorned with a star that shone with iridescent silver ink. Struck by its reference to the night sky she'd just been watching, she tried to remember what book it was. *Astronomy text?* she wondered. No, she recalled. That one was taller and thinner.

Curious now, she stood and withdrew the heavy volume. Touching the front cover—where an even larger star had been pressed into the leather   she recognized the *Illuminated Bible.* She'd bought it a few years earlier, not so much for the words as for the uniqueness of its artwork: richly foiled lettering and borders in a Old-World style seldom practiced in modern-day computerized printing.

The book had a special appeal tonight, and before retiring, she decided to read the Christmas story. She pushed back against the sofa cushions and settled the tome on her lap.

Opening the front cover, she heard the creak of the binding and inhaled the aroma of fine leather.

A page introducing the King James edition read:

> "For whereas it was the expectation of many, who wished not well unto our *Sion*, that upon the setting of that bright *Occidental Star*, Queen *Elizabeth* of most happy memory, some thick and palpable clouds of darkness would so have overshadowed this Land, that men should have been in doubt which way they were to walk. . . ."

For a few moments Miranda's mind drifted away on implications of courtly intrigue that seemed to contrast sharply with the tireless dedication of monks poring over their translations. And then she noticed something else—again, a mention of "star," and a reference to "clouds of darkness."

Nothing featured a star so clearly as the Christmas story itself. So, skipping the Old Testament, she carefully turned the gilt-edged pages to Matthew—the Christmas story would be here somewhere. Reading a few verses, she found herself growing sleepy. *Maybe I can find it tomorrow,* she mused. About to close the book, she changed her mind. *Why not try opening to a random page to see if something catches my eye?* It was an interesting technique she sometimes used with other texts—the writings of Lao Tsu or the *I Ching.* She might find something interesting to think about as she drifted off to sleep.

Pausing to meditate a moment, she then carefully grasped a segment of pages, flipped them, then dropped her finger on a verse. "Do not sleep, as do others," it said. Arrested by what she saw, she felt a twinge of that strange urgency that had plagued her all afternoon.

What does this mean? she asked herself. But the answer was already staring her in the face. Whether she liked it or not, it seemed very clear she'd received orders from the Universe *not* to go to sleep.

That's what I get for asking, she pouted. *On the other hand, maybe I really have tuned in to something larger.* As with the case of her mountainscape painting, just because she didn't yet understand it, didn't mean she wouldn't in the future. For now, she apparently had both the responsibility and the privilege of a midnight vigil.

As a former crew member of the ship *Phoenix* on a voyage to save whales, she'd taken late watch a few times. Those had been magical nights, when the planet seemed to yield at least a few of its secrets. Perhaps tonight would be the same.

The only recurring image of the last few minutes was star—the stars in the night sky, the silver star embossed on the Bible, and the mention of "star" in that opening text. *Does that mean I'm supposed to add a star to the image?* She couldn't see how that would work, though, since this was a day-time image.

In any case, she still had a long night in front of her. How could she fill the hours? Probably not with painting. She'd done so much in the last few days, she'd temporarily used up her inspiration. Besides, it almost seemed that painting tonight would be too personal, too selfish a pursuit. She'd been *asked*—no, *told*—to stay awake. There had to be a higher purpose than her own.

In that case, what could she do to further the cause of harmony, of "on Earth peace, good will to man"? If ever there was a night for such reflections, surely it would be the night before Christmas Eve. Reaching for her scratchpad, she flipped to a blank page and opened the cap of her green fountain pen. Lists of images came to mind—some that she'd painted already, some she hadn't. *These are the holiday cards I did,* she thought. *They could be a set of cards for charity.*

As the idea sank in, it seemed an inspiration. *Yes! I could sell them for full retail, but donate all but the cost to one of the environmental organizations. Maybe Heal the Bay or NRDC. I should ask Sam; maybe she wants help with her new Pier project.* Miranda thought some more about what to paint. *All those birds I did for the Duck Stamp Competition—they could become a set of cards.*

The prize she'd coveted for so long suddenly seemed unimportant in light of a new, worthier goal. Soon the energy that had drained earlier was replenished from a new wellspring, and Miranda retrieved a sketchpad, resumed her place on the sofa, and drew images into the wee hours.

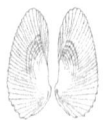

Chapter 4

The day before Christmas Eve dawned over the mountains and was shining first-light through Miranda's window when she woke with a start. Still on the sofa, she'd fallen asleep with her sketchpad on her lap. Now that she thought about it, laying the drawing pencil on the coffee table was the last thing she remembered doing.

She glanced at the clock, and then around the room. The anxiety of the previous night had faded. All the details of the large room, from overhead beams to shining floors, from sparkling window lights to gleaming table—all seemed infused with a special glow. The aspect of everything she saw and felt was so changed, she could almost believe Santa had made his overnight visit.

Among Miranda's very favorite things to cook were her "watercolor pancakes." A personal invention dating back to her childhood, the from-scratch endeavor never failed to call forth some of the sweetest of her memories, including the Christmas morning her mother announced that her younger daughter— then aged twelve—had transformed the family kitchen into an artist-chef's atelier. Miranda had then proudly presented multi-colored stacks of pancakes to her patiently waiting family. Overlooking the uneven sizes and occasional lumps, her parents and even her sister has praised her efforts, giving her a quick round of applause before the wares were sampled.

Giggling at the recollection, Miranda set about step two in her process: dividing her pancake batter into four equal batches, then spooning in the pre-mixed homemade vegetable dye food coloring she'd prepared a week earlier. She chuckled again as one bowl's contents turned pink, the next pale green, the next sky-blue, and that last a vivid yellow.

By the time Sally bustled in with her tray of spices and a dozen eggs, making herself at home in Miranda's kitchen, the doorbell rang again to admit both Samantha and Kevin. Sam carried her fresh fruit salad to the counter, added some vanilla yogurt, then carried her beautiful serving bowl directly to the dining area.

"Miranda, your table looks fabulous!" she enthused. "Those dishes! Where did you find them? And those darling pine-tree linens? And the miniature trees for your centerpiece?"

"Oh, here and there," Miranda called, winking at Sally.

"Want the sausages to go in that cast iron skillet?" Kevin asked.

"Yup. All ready for you."

"They're pre-cooked, just need to be warmed up a little," he explained, washing his hands in the kitchen sink.

Sally's sunny side up eggs were now nestled in Miranda's largest Chantal skillet, bubbling and popping invitingly, while Miranda began flipping the first of her pancakes on the electric griddle she'd plugged in farther down the counter to give her cooking guests room to work.

Ten minutes later, everyone served themselves, admiring Sally's red-and-green sprinkled "Christmas Eggs," Kevin's plump apple-sausages, Sam's fruit salad, and Miranda's home-made flapjacks.

When plates had been carried to the table and the gustatory offerings admired, the four friends took a moment to hold hands and give thanks—for the season, for the friendships, and—in the case of Sally and Sam—for the holiday cease-fire.

"They really are watercolor pancakes," Sally cooed, "just like you said. Moon in the mornin', however did you think o' such a thing?"

"Mind of a child," Miranda replied shyly.

"Heart of an artist," Sam contradicted.

"Should we eat them, or frame them?" Kevin asked with his customary candor.

Everyone laughed. Then, everyone ate.

Miranda had to admit the holiday brunch had been a smashing success. Since they'd all agreed they wouldn't exchange gifts as part of their celebration today, the only offerings her guests had brought were consumable, now indeed mostly consumed. They'd manage to create their own tradition this first year in her new home—one she hoped they'd repeat through the years.

Samantha cleared the table—commenting again on the charming mugs with their coastal pines pattern marching around each—while Sally insisted on doing the dishes, and the kitchen soon looked clean enough for a showroom. Digesting their repast, Kevin sat comfortably on her couch, his long legs stretching well beyond her trunk-coffee-table, Shadow curled in his lap, the two of them dozing in an apparent pancake stupor.

Sam and Sally—still on their best behavior toward each other today—perused the art hung on various walls, ooh-ing and ahh-ing at their hostess's talent. And then the guests all bid fond farewells, leaving Shadow now snuggled against a pillow, and Miranda glancing around the magically spotless dining room and kitchen.

Her plan for the rest of the afternoon was to finish packing, and then take the evening shift at Finder's Gallery. This would give Nicole a chance to run out for some dinner before returning to the shop to close for the holiday.

Miranda headed down to her bedroom then glanced around to look at her suitcase. To her surprise, she found Shadow sitting atop the bag as if waiting to be packed along with her other belongings.

"How do you always know, Kitty? How do you know I'm about to pack for a trip?"

"Ow," Shadow answered, her expression somewhere between irritation and loneliness.

"I won't be gone long, you know. And Kevin promised to take care of you. You'll get to ride in the car when he takes me to the airport, then go home with him."

Her cat merely blinked, eyes like amber jewels winking in black velvet.

"Oh, come here." Miranda lifted the soft little body into her arms, then listened to the loud purring that hummed like a soft motor. When she put her down on the bed, she added, "We can play the packing game. One of your favorites."

For brunch, she'd worn her holiday sweater with its pattern of dark green pines against a burgundy background, since it complimented her table decor. But for tonight, she chose her star-patterned sweater, which brought back to mind the theme of her previous night's study.

She flipped her long hair over the collar, decided the burgundy jeans still worked, slipped into comfortable flats, then checked herself in the mirror, adding a touch of maroon lipstick and fastening her hair in a silver clip.

Shadow watched as Miranda drew clothes from the closet to make a pre-packing array across the bed. "I have to take the long green dress, of course," she explained. "Mother and Mer would both expect it, and the color is perfect for Christmas. And that means I need the silver jewelry, the green flats, and . . . I still can't find that green suede purse. Oh, and I better take boots. There's gonna be snow in New York."

Unsure whether she prattled on to sooth the kitty, or herself, Miranda gathered her clothing until the blouses and sweaters, underwear and slacks, stocking, shoes, and toiletries were all assembled. Within the hour, she'd arranged them in her suitcase, which she hauled up the stairs, Shadow following.

"Well, Kitty, the only other thing I need is my coat, and I'll get that out of the hall closet in the morning. Now, I need to get over to the gallery. See you later for supper, okay?"

"Meh," the cat replied, then marched herself back to her favorite spot on the couch.

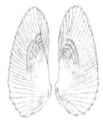

Chapter 5

Miranda found Finders Gallery bustling with holiday fervor when she arrived, and Nicole glanced over at her with an expression of relief and gratitude.

Seeing her friend engaged with a customer at the moment, Miranda slipped into the back room to stow her purse, then stepped behind the selling counter to review the current inventory notebook, which separated the works by artist and included bios, price lists, and special notations.

She couldn't resist flipping to her own section to refresh her memory as to which of her paintings were currently on display. *Pacific Laps, You Otter Sea Me Play, Pining Over the Water, Do Hummers Dream, Sea Our Christmas Ball.* She calculated briefly—two wildlife pieces and three landscapes, and was considering whether she should talk with Zelda about what other works should be here, when the door chimed and customers entered. Smiling automatically as she looked up, she greeted a holiday-dressed couple, and began answering questions.

An hour later, the gallery suddenly emptied, and Nicole finally had a chance to greet her friend.

"Oh, Miranda," she began in her Montreal accent, "I cannot even *begin* to thank you for coming in!"

"Happy I could help! Least I could do is give you a dinner break, considering you have several of my own pieces on display."

"Bien sur!" Nicole replied, confirming that, of course, the gallery would be showing her pieces.

"And I did go through the list of the other artists paintings and prints, so I can answer questions . . . though not as expertly as you would. Anything you need me to do?"

Nicole considered for a moment. *"No . . . je n'crois pas.* I don't think so. Ah, oui! I would love it if you would wrap the print for Lorraine Larimer. You 'ave such a beautiful way, n'est pas?"

"I don't know about that, but I'd be happy to wrap a gift for the head of our Town Council."

"Exactement," she confirmed in French. "Anyway, I will not be long. Just I want to get a bowl of chowder with baguette from Michael's. I'll return as quickly as I can."

"Good choice. And please, take your time," Miranda reassured. "I'll enjoy being here."

"Merci, Miranda. Merci milles fois!"

And with her "thousand" thank you's, Nicole was out the door.

The dinner hour had apparently taken over Milford-Haven, creating a lull in the gallery. Miranda took the opportunity to straighten the disordered prints in their bins, pick up the empty coffee cup someone had left on a window sill, and rearrange some of the smaller art pieces.

With the customer spaces in good order, she decided to check the back room in case she could help Nicole by restoring a bit of order. Absorbed with alphabetizing-by-artist the stored prints, she lost track of time.

She suddenly realized it'd been several minutes since she'd checked out front, to see who might be browsing. She'd been listening for the bell placed on the customer counter, but hadn't heard it ring. Still, it was time to check. While she was heading toward the front desk, she figured she might as well carry the box of replacement wrapping paper to replenish the supply. The box was a bit heavy as well as being large and awkward. Holding it in both arms, she spun around to use her backside to press open the door marked "Employees Only" as wide as possible. When her hind quarters met with an obstruction she was so startled, she nearly dropped the burden to the floor.

"Oh!" she said.

"Oh!" called a male voice.

She'd backed into a customer, she realized, a male customer, making rather too much contact with a stranger. She inhaled an aroma—some combination of pine and spice, an alchemical mixture whose molecules seemed to slide into pre-determined places along the strands of her DNA. She felt her pulse stutter as she spun once again. She found herself drawn into a penetrating stare.

"Terribly sorry," she gasped.

"No, I apologize. I shouldn't have—" the man began.

"I was just—" she interrupted.

"—been peering into your—" he tried to continue.

"—about to hang the sign—" She said, then smiled. Instead of smiling back, the man seemed transfixed, and Miranda watched as his deep sapphire eyes seemed to darken almost to navy. Then a smile began to play at the edges of his mouth. She felt her own pulse begin to surge, her cheeks to grow warm.

"I r-really should learn to stop walking backward," she stammered. "As my mother has often mentioned."

Mara Purl

"Your mother?" he asked, frowning with evident confusion. "Mrs. Jones," she explained.

"Jones?"

"No, it's not about my mother. I just...." Her words trailed off. *Falling. I'm falling into those eyes. Why is he looking at me that way? As if . . . he'd been looking for me. Well, he found me. I'm here. I'm found.*

"So, I, uh," he stammered, "I did find something I'd like to purchase."

"Oh!" she said, shaking herself as though from a dream and relieved to move past the inexplicably awkward moment.

The man, still looking at her, forced a smile. "Yeah, it'll be a perfect gift for Christmas. For *my* mother."

"Your mother?"

"Mrs. Smith."

"I'm glad," she said, then gave him her best customer smile. "Which painting?"

At his gesture, she followed him into the gallery display, then gave another small smile when he identified the piece, which she removed from its hooks.

Back at her work station on the far side of the front counter, she opened a notebook, flipped to a tab and drew her finger down a column of figures, though her muddled brain couldn't make sense of the familiar figures until she did so again.

Focusing on the immediate tasks, she ran his credit card, handed him the receipt to sign, then watched as he lifted the painting as if to leave with it. "No wrapping?" she asked.

"I'll take care of it. Thanks, though." He kept staring, then added, "So that's your name, then? Jones?"

"Right. One of them." She gave him a half smile, this time. "Smith," he said, though she'd already gathered as much from his credit card.

To be polite, she stuck a hand over the counter to grab one of his. "Nice to meet you, Mr. Smith."

He flinched slightly at the touch.

Startled, she pulled away, then walked around the counter to him. Now it was her turn to study his eyes, noticing a tightness around them. With utmost care, she gently took both his hands in hers, then turned them over, inhaling sharply when she saw that welts crossed his palms.

"Yeah," he said in explanation. "I had an adventure today." Intuitively, she knew what that adventure must have been. When she raised her eyes back to his, she wanted to take him minute by minute through her odd painting project—the series of compulsions to fill the small canvass with the unfamiliar image, the sense of urgency she hadn't understood, but had simply trusted.

Worry must have been written all over her face, because he suddenly blurted out, "I'm okay."

"I'm so very glad." Relief riffled through her like a warm breeze. She let go of his hands—and of the notion that words could explain what she'd experienced in her studio. Instead, she added simply, "And apparently I have another painting for you."

Gesturing to him to wait a moment, she dashed into the back room, then returned carrying a desk-top easel and a small, unframed canvas. She placed in on the counter, and watched as his gaze fixed on her latest work.

She continued to stare as his gaze tracked across the details she knew so well: the storm crowding the mountain top; benches traced with icy snow cut into a steep cliff, and then the rope, hanging as if from nowhere down the sheer rock face.

I have to be leaving soon," she declared. "But you have to tell me the story."

Milford-Haven Recipes
Miranda's Holiday Breakfast
Watercolor Pancakes

2 cups whole milk

2 cups unbleached all-purpose flour

2 Tbsp sugar

2 tsp baking powder

½ tsp baking soda

½ tsp salt

1 egg (preferably large)

3 Tbsp melted butter (preferably unsalted)

4 batches of organic food coloring (see next recipes)

1. Wet Ingredients – whisk together milk, egg and melted butter. Set aside.

2. Dry Ingredients – whisk together flour, sugar, baking powder, baking soda and salt. Make a well in the center, pour in wet mixture and gently combine with wooden spoon, without over mixing.

3. Divide batter into 4 different bowls. Add 1 teaspoon of color into one bowl each, tinting batter into 4 shades.

4. On a heated griddle, spray or brush 1 teaspoon of oil. (Griddle is heated properly when water drops bounce.) Pour ¼ cup of batter onto separate areas then cook until large bubbles appear over entire surface of the pancake. Then flip and cook for about 1 more minute.

5. Keep pancakes warm until everyone can be served.

6. Service with real butter and organic maple syrup. Or, service with real butter, confectioner's sugar and sprinkles.

Organic Food Coloring
(As created by Leite's Culinaris est. 1999)

Note: the vegetables in these recipes will create pastel "watercolor" colors, rather than vibrant shades.

Pink
¼ cup canned beets, drained
1 tsp juice from the can
Blend ingredients at high speed until smooth. Add 1 teaspoon to batter, and more as needed for desired color.

Yellow
¼ cup water
½ cup ground tumeric
Boil ingredients in small saucepan for 3-5 minutes, then cool. Add 1 teaspoon to batter, and more as needed for color. (Note that tumeric stains fingers & countertops.)

Purple
⅓ cup blueberries, drained, fresh or frozen
2 tsp water
Blend ingredients at high speed until smooth. Strain the skins. Add 1 teaspoon to batter, and more as needed for desired color.

Green
1 cup spinach, drained, fresh or frozen
3 Tbsp water
Blend ingredients at high speed until smooth. Strain and cool. Add 1 teaspoon to batter, and more as needed for desired color.

To achieve more colors, experiment with blending the above recipes! Note these natural dyes can be stored in your refrigerator for up to two weeks in small glass bottles.

Return soon to . . .
Milford-Haven!
Available now . . .

Mara Purl's
Where an Angel's On a Rope

A Holiday novella
in the exciting Milford-Haven saga

Enjoy the following Preview
from the novelette . . .

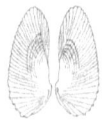

Prologue

A red sun lurked below the winter skyline, ready to bathe the Angeles Crest in ruby light.

Standing at the mountain's pinnacle, the mighty stag used powerful neck muscles to tilt his antler array at the pale moon, as though he could tumble it down to the horizon far below.

Long and branched, the antlers caught the first ray of sun even before the summit illuminated. Were a Chumash celebrant nearby, he would honor the sacred deer, recognizing its presence as an early harbinger of spring.

Yet now, just past the December solstice, the stag hid in its native forest, bare deciduous boughs conspiring to conceal those arcing antlers, groundcover absorbing traces of hoof marks.

No human, ancient or modern, would cross the stag's path in this protected forest. As though sensing his increased visibility in the dawn, the creature snorted, stamped his foot, and made his way across the top of his favorite peak.

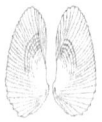

Chapter 1

Cornelius Smith found nothing about Christmas appealed to him.

At least, not in the usual sense. A man of science, he found the Christmas Season to be a time of superstition and exaggeration, of hyperbole and overspending; a time given to the cheap commercialization of symbols now so distant and misinterpreted as to have been rendered meaningless.

Sitting high in the driver's seat of his Dodge Durango, he crept as quietly as the vehicle would allow down the still-slumbering Main Street. He allowed that, at five a.m. on this otherwise bleak morning the day before Christmas Eve, the decorative lights had some charm: the huge window panes of Finders Gallery were filled with multi-colored glass sculptures—all lit from behind, sending forth a rainbow of light into the darkened lane.

He slowed enough to peer into a store called Shell Shock, which he didn't remember seeing before. In its window stood a Christmas tree made entirely of seashells, with a large star fish adorning its top. When he came to By The Book bookshop—

which had been there as long as Cornelius could remember—
he brought his vehicle to a stop and idled while he took in the
details. This year, the owner had created an extraordinary diorama. A miniature street from Charles Dickens's London ex-
tended across the interior of the large-paned window, complete
with tiny horses and carriages, doll-citizens in top hats and
bonnets, and among the storefronts, he saw the Little Dorrit
Book Shop. *Charles Dickens himself would recognize the street
in a trice.*

But soon enough, daylight would begin to wash over the
town of Milford-Haven, revealing the artificiality of its gaudy
displays, and Cornelius felt eager to leave it all behind for a day.
Come tomorrow, he'd be joining his parents for all the merri-
ment of the season, and he had to admit he'd enjoy it for their
sakes. But for him, the finest winter had to offer was the deep
quiet of falling snow, the hollow thud of a heavy branch dropping
its sodden weight, the pulsing, wet nose of a doe foraging for
food. All these delights hovered far from civilization, and he
edged his car onto California Highway 1.

Watching the last of the town disappear in his rearview
mirror, he shook his head at the garish blinking of a neon motel
sign. *Folks just need to make a living,* he could hear his father
say. For Cornelius, the living was eked out from the dribbles and
drabs of government grants. Though employed by NASA, his lot
as a scientist was forever having to prove the worth of his ex-
periments in practical applications. Fewer and fewer were the
opportunities for pure research—another sad commentary on
today's world.

How could a scientist look for something he didn't yet
know existed? The most startling discoveries were often made
"by accident"—though he considered that to be a misnomer.

Accidental finds were in fact serendipitous discovery—and one had to be living a life of curiosity and open-mindedness in order to notice the anomaly that so often signaled hidden treasure.

As he turned his head, his eye caught the movement of the angel hanging from his rearview mirror, and he snorted at himself in the green glow of his dashboard lights. It was his one concession to childhood Christmases—the little stained glass angel his mother had given him long ago. In her honor, he dutifully hung it in his car every December, her birthday month—and his. Dangling from its tiny gold rope, it swayed now with open arms, holding a star in one hand. *Well, Mom*, he thought, *the joke's on me.*

Though he knew the roads well enough, whenever possible Cornelius used stellar navigation, trusting the stars more than Earth-based information. Craning his neck out the driver's-side window, he took his bearings. Clear skies, four-fifteen a.m., Pacific Standard Time: Ursa Majoris, with a level dipper, should be high overhead, with Orion the hunter just finishing his leap lower in the Western sky. *Check*, he said to himself.

Although he'd intended using the stars only to help him negotiate the mere ripples on a small planet in a familiar solar system, he found he could not easily shut off the exercise of mentally expanding the view from his present location. To the west, Mars shone brightly in the sky. *Where is Jupiter now?* he asked himself, the answer coming almost immediately—*off my right toe.* Calculating that if he drew a line from himself to Jupiter, it would pass through the constellation Pavonus—The Peacock—in the southern hemisphere.

Two hours later, Cornelius steadied the steering wheel while sipping fresh coffee from his travel mug. His visor shielded his eyes from the blaze of sun blasting over the edge of the eastern mountains. Having checked the map, he pleasured in the surge of the Durango's powerful engine as it labored up into the foothills.

As his vehicle climbed through 3,000 feet, he glanced at the car's digital clock—6:49 a.m. He looked to his left in time to see the full moon, now a disk of luminous tissue hung on a floating curtain of pale lavender. He chuckled. *As if she's peering over the western slopes, caught in her gossamer peignoir.* Now he stole a glance to the right. Through gaps between the mountains, a red haze lifted off the eastern horizon.

Normally, the rising sun signaled the end of his workday, so he got a thrill from the feeling he was playing hooky by having a daylight adventure. In cities, artists claimed the night for their own. He imagined jazz musicians sequestered in smoky clubs, and actors peeling off greasepaint in the wee hours. In the wild, the night was the purview of nocturnal hunters padding on huge, silent feet through forest and ravine.

But, for the astronomer, night was simply the closest thing to reality one could get while being Earth-bound. Daylight existed as an inconvenient maintenance function the planet needed to regenerate her ecosystem. Like a cloak Earth had to wear to mask her identity, blue sky concealed her context and location, and blocked out neighbors both near and far, leaving her isolated in her lonely corner of space. Passionate about his work, Cornelius usually found himself impatient for the dimming of the intrusive rays from that nearest star so he could be about his nightly tasks.

But the season invited breaks in routine with celebrations of many kinds, and he did enjoy visiting the little church for Christmas service with his parents. However, today he would follow a secret tradition of celebrating Christmas in his own way. If there were a ceremony he would choose to join, it would probably be the Chumash Winter Solstice—a time of quiet contemplation and deep silences, even in the midst of large gatherings. But he would celebrate with rocks and trees, and with largely unseen animal companions whom he would do his best not to disturb.

As Cornelius continued to follow the snaking highway, the mountains seemed to welcome him like relatives at a family reunion. As though they'd posted sentinels to guide him home, thick brown yucca spires sprouted from prickly ruffs at even intervals along the roadside. Passing a sign that read *Double Fine,* he laughed—indeed, that's just how things were today: *double* fine.

As he climbed through 5,000 feet, the colors of dawn were shifting so rapidly they proved hard to describe. *It really looks like a painting. In fact, I remember seeing one with clouds something like this.* In a gallery in Milford-Haven, he'd noticed the work of the local artist Miranda Jones, a painter of wildlife and nature scenes. He tried to imagine how she'd interpret the mountains in front of him now. The ridges closest to him were mottled browns, but just one ridge away, they mysteriously took on an azure blue cast. She'd know how to capture them, he thought, marveling at the artistic talent beyond his ken.

Then he caught a familiar sight—a gleaming white observatory crouched in a metal forest of broadcast towers. The place was incalculably rich in astronomical history. From here, Michaelson and Morley had bounced light off the nearby Mt. Baldy, the highest peak in the region. When they used the terrain as a natural reflecting device, their results led directly to Einstein's Theory of Relativity.

As if this weren't enough, it was here, on a mountain top overlooking Los Angeles, that the first hundred-inch telescope had been built in 1918. And sixty years ago, looking through that very lens, Hubble discovered the universe was expanding.

The universe has expanded over 340 trillion miles since then, he calculated, *and that's not including Einstein's acceleration theory. Time flies.* Laughing at his joke, he realized how true that little aphorism had proven in his own life. As a grad student, he'd spent over 150 nights at Mt. Wilson, peering at the night sky, tracking the spinning cosmos. *That was a long time ago . . . and it was only yesterday.*

Return soon to . . .

Milford-Haven!

Available now . . .

Mara Purl's
Whose Angel Key Rings

A Holiday Novella
in the exciting Milford-Haven saga

Enjoy the following Preview
from the novel . . .

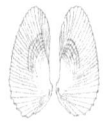

Prologue

The sun hung over the horizon like a burnished red Christmas ornament ready to drop into the Pacific with a final sizzle.

At the Calma estate high on the Santa Barbara mountainside, nothing was left of the holiday but an embarrassment of torn wrappings, empty boxes, and the lingering aromas of dinner. The home itself seemed overhung with an enchanted slumber.

James Hughes was the only person still awake. Now that he was in his late sixties, he carried a little extra weight on his five-foot-eleven frame. Though his gray hair had thinned, his brown eyes were keen as ever, and his voice still rang with a soft-spoken mid-Atlantic accent, despite his many years in America.

Estate Manager, majordomo, confidante—he'd been called many things over the years, from butler to family friend. Though he had never presumed to call himself a relation, his protective instincts were certainly familial.

He knew both the Calvin men had settled into a sleep saturated with the best meal of the year and the spirit of the day. Quietly mounting the stairs, he peered into Joseph Calvin's room. Just as he suspected, the master had again fallen asleep with his reading glasses on. Removing them with the utmost care, James placed them on the nightstand, switched off the bedside lamp, and left the room as quietly as he'd entered.

Downstairs in the den, James discovered Zackery quietly snoring before the last glow of a dying fire. Draping a throw across the man he still thought of as the "young master," James turned out the table lamp.

He decided to leave on the Christmas tree lights in case Zackery woke during the wee hours. Passing through the kitchen, James looked over the polished surfaces and clicked off all but the small table lamp by the phone, then left by the back door.

Fog swirled over the stone path leading to his own cottage, which sent a welcoming glow into the dark chill. The whole of the mountain seemed shrouded by a dense cloud, the lights of Santa Barbara nothing more than a faint luminosity, as distant as the rush of waves hitting the shore far below.

James opened his front door, then closed it behind him, relieved both to recover his sense of privacy and to be off-the-clock. When he'd completed his evening ablutions, he pulled on his comfortable robe and worn slippers, then sat in his favorite chair to enjoy reading some Charles Dickens before retiring for the night. But reading proved impossible.

Nestled in his breast pocket, a small, vivid presence would not be ignored. Reaching inside, he retrieved the golden key ring and turned it over in his hand. More durable than dainty, exquisitely crafted, it was an assembly of three small treasures: a ring incised with a pattern of waves; a tiny, plump angel of puffed gold; and an ornately embossed key.

She'd entrusted it to him so many years ago, the late Mrs. Calvin, and he'd known exactly where to find it when the time came. But then it went missing from its special hiding place, and now—just as mysteriously—it had returned. He hoped its sudden appearance hinted not at the handiwork of fickle Fate but, instead—as promised—signified the stately grace of Providence.

To ponder this possibility, he sat quietly, reviewing the events of the family's most momentous Christmas in recent memory.

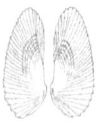

Chapter 1

Christmas morning dawned, tapping on the windows of Zackery Calvin's villa like a pesky elf. Irritated to be wakened so early, Zack squinted at the color leaking into his room. The elf, not content to be spirited away with Santa in the night, apparently lingered to paint the sky a bright Christmas red.

Paintbrush . . . Miranda. Miranda Jones, painter and heartbreaker. Couldn't he avoid thinking about her for one day? Zack twisted in his sheets. *Well, you certainly made a fine mess of that,* he berated himself. She was someone special who'd come into his life but, obviously, he hadn't had the slightest idea what to do about her. And as if that weren't enough, his indecision and ineptitude had apparently trampled on Cynthia's feelings as well. She'd made that clear by taking back everything she'd ever given him. He'd have to tiptoe around her at brunch today, sublimating his own feelings—whatever they were—disenfranchised in his own home.

Christmas morning was supposed to be a time of magical anticipation. Zack yanked the covers over his head and plunged himself back into the oblivion of sleep.

Cynthia Radcliffe awakened Christmas morning determined to make a new start. Her eyes red from having cried herself to sleep, she started a pot of dark roast with cinnamon. After standing in a hot shower, she pulled on her cheeriest red sweatshirt and pants, then added a pair of Santa socks to keep her feet cozy in the chilly air.

Better I'm alone today, she thought, *no need to act the bright, Christmas nymph.* But almost immediately, second thoughts swirled through her brain like the cream she stirred into her coffee. She could still go. She could be dressing now for brunch with Zackery. But the smart thing was still to turn him down. A woman had to have her pride.

Thanksgiving two years ago. The uninvited images began surfacing again—their first meeting, their instant attraction, their outrageous flirtations. And then a wildly erotic romance that almost overspilled the boundaries of decency. Just before they'd have celebrated their second Thanksgiving together, he seemed mysteriously to fall off the edge of the world. Whether there was someone else, or whether this was just typical Zackery cowardice, she didn't really know. The call had come not from him, but from James. In the most *polite* language, she'd been invited to retrieve her belongings.

Fine. She'd made a clean sweep of his rooms a month ago. She'd packed everything she'd taken there and every single thing she'd added to his cottage at Calma. Not that she'd *needed* all of it—the boxes were still in her closet, unopened.

When the Christmas brunch invitation came a week ago—left as a message on her answering machine, no less!—it had seemed perfunctory, as though Zackery didn't have anything *better* to do, and as though he took it for granted she'd be there. The tone in his voice wasn't nearly contrite enough. If he wanted to apologize and make amends, he'd have to be enthusiastic about it. But he didn't suggest a romantic reconciliation. Instead, he asked her to "join the family at Calma." *The family?* That could only mean the two Calvin men, junior and senior—brooding pouts from one, small talk from the other.

Then Zelda called, wondering what Cynthia would be wearing. *So Zelda was invited. How did she know I was?* She answered her own question. *She's certainly wormed her way into the good graces of Zackery's father in short order.* But that might not be a bad thing. Zelda was at least a *sometime* ally—and not someone Cynthia wanted as an enemy.

At first, Zelda even talked her into accepting. "Far better to look gorgeous, tantalize him for two hours, then leave for 'another engagement.'" Zelda's counsel had always been sound before. Cynthia just didn't have the energy to pull it off. And a personal appearance with tear-puffed eyes would only make her look pathetic.

Pouring more hot coffee into her cup, she walked to the storage closet and flung open the door. Yanking boxes from their hiding places, she dragged them all to the middle of her living room floor and opened their folded lids. It was time to rout the dark corners of her affair with Zackery Calvin. She'd start with these boxes.

Peering into the first one, she couldn't seem to make sense of its contents. A small bottle of tarragon with some rolled-up stockings; aspirin and cough medicine with books; make-up with a pair of running shoes; her scarves with a bottle of Chinese plum sauce. The matching bathrobes were in one box, but their ties were in another.

The extent of the disorder surprised even her. *What was I thinking?* Cynthia asked herself. At the time, she'd been so overwrought she simply hurled things into whatever was handy. *Best not to remember.*

Return soon to . . .

Milford-Haven!

Available now . . .

Mara Purl's
When the Heart Listens

a prequel novella

in the exciting Milford-Haven saga

Enjoy the following Preview . . .

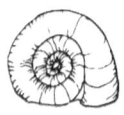

Chapter 1

Veronica Jones lifted the monogrammed napkin from her lap and touched it to the corners of her mouth. Folding the smooth cloth in half, she pulled it through the silver napkin ring that bore the same initials as the linen.

The sun room where she and her husband—and their daughters, when they were home—usually shared breakfast felt chilly but cheerful with early forsythia blooms in the garden emanating vivid yellow through French doors and tall windows.

Veri, as her family and friends called her, looked across the small table at her husband of many years—still handsome and straight-backed, the gray at his temples lending a distinguished touch to his sculpted face.

"I've got to do something about the girls," she said, eyeing the coffee pot and considering whether she'd allow herself another half cup.

"You're always doing something about the girls," Charles said, not even looking over the top of the San Francisco Chronicle he read religiously every morning.

"You know what I mean, Charles. One is living in that icy tower of glass; the other is practically buried in that basement. Neither of them is truly happy. Neither is really safe."

Charles folded his paper and looked into her eyes. "Don't fret, dear. They're grown women, now. You can't live their lives for them. You can't tell them what to do."

From his mollifying tone, and from the softness of his expression, she knew he sympathized. Still, his words rankled. She couldn't bear the idea of not being able to help her daughters—whether or not they asked. She had, in fact, come up with a plan. Well, a partial plan. Though she had no intention of revealing details to their father just yet, she did think a mention might be politic.

"Uh-oh," he said, shaking his head while he poured himself a fresh cup of coffee. "You're up to something. Let's have it."

"Well," she began, "it would save them both money, and they'd be far more secure."

Veri smiled, and when her husband squinted, she saw with satisfaction that amusement was already beginning to coax a smile at the edges of his mouth.

Good. I'll make him my co-conspirator before he even knows what he's sanctioning.

Meredith Jones pressed the button for 22 and closed her eyes as a gust of wind swirled through the lobby and sent a blast into the elevator. April breezes howled through the shaft until the doors fully closed, and she felt her heart lurch right along with the car as it climbed through the lower floors.

With a "ding," the doors flew open and she stepped onto the faux-marble floor, then clacked down the hallway to her unit, wrinkling her nose at the cooking smells that clung to the wallpaper in the corridor. Sliding the key into her lock, she pushed open her door and flung off her high heels even before the metal front door slammed shut behind her.

"Ahh," she said aloud, dropping her briefcase, throwing her coat over the back of a bar stool, and opening the fridge. She reached inside for a half-finished bottle of Chardonnay, poured herself a glass, then settled on the sofa, wiggling her toes as she stretched her legs across the cushions.

Missed it again, she said, bemoaning that she never managed to get home in time to see the sunset. *But what little I saw from the car was gorgeous.*

For a new VP of client relations at a high-powered financial management firm, working late came with the territory. Still, she felt entitled to complain in the privacy of her own apartment. When her stomach rumbled, she remembered that bellyaching wouldn't put food on her table.

"Pizza Palace?" she wondered aloud. They did have a great Italian salad. Sezchuan Sensations sounded more appealing, though, and she stepped to the kitchen counter, picked up the handset with her favorite restaurants programmed into the speed-dial function, and placed the call.

By the time she'd changed into her dove-gray sweat pants and zippered top, prepared a tray, and turned on her TV, the intercom began buzzing.

A few minutes later, while she deftly picked at her Szechuan chicken and spicy string beans, she rewound the tape in her VCR and hit play, laughing out loud when Kramer, looking as if he'd just stuck his finger in an electrical outlet, walked across the hall and into Jerry's apartment to ask an inane question. It was a show about . . . nothing, Meredith decided, which was why she enjoyed watching it. How else could she take her mind off the daily stress and unwind?

Suddenly the crisp bite of spicy chicken trapped between her chop sticks didn't look as delicious as it had a moment earlier. *I've managed to avoid thinking about it for a whole hour and half, and now it's back, dammit.*

Albert Rothman, recently named senior partner—and the youngest ever to be so named—knew how brilliant he was, how valuable to the firm, and he had his eye on wealth to rival sultans. But he had a blind spot about his sex appeal. Convinced any woman would be grateful to be blessed by his attentions, he'd so far managed only to offend "lesser" employees, each of whom had been quietly dismissed with an attractive financial bonus. And Meredith only knew about these arrangements because she herself had now made partner.

Today, however, he'd managed to offend her twice, in two distinct ways. First, he'd questioned her data interpretation at her debut partner presentation. Though it'd stung, she'd accepted the criticism graciously, acknowledging the new alpha dog, flattering him by treating him as leader, though in truth he was only a couple of years older than she.

Second, he'd propositioned her. *Talk about a no-win scenario,* Meredith thought bitterly. She knew perfectly well how the game was played: be charming, but not overtly flirtatious; dress in a way that was appealing but not sexy; do your work better than any of the male partners.

A mentor had once said to her, "Meredith, in this business you have to be either very good, or very bad." She hadn't understood what he meant at first, so he'd explained. "If you plan to sleep your way to the top, be strategic and don't get emotionally involved. If you don't plan to use sex to get ahead, be sure not to sleep with anyone to get ahead. It'll be used against you."

Best advice I ever got, she mused. She'd adhered to his suggestion, and never dated anyone at the firm. In fact, she felt professional behavior at work was the gold standard. She also felt that what she did on her own time was her own business.

She glanced at her chopsticks as though she had no idea what to do with them and set them aside as her thoughts came back to Albert. Their paths were entwined at work. Would she be interested in dating him if not? Her instincts told her he was too self-involved and though too little of women to truly hold her interest. In any case, because of their work connection, the point was moot. Her own personal rules wouldn't allow involvement with him.

So where did that leave her now? *Damned if I do, damned if I don't.* If she turned him down, he'd take offence, and try his best to take it out of her career performance, one way or another. If she accepted his invitation—drink and dinner for now, but who knows what he really expected—she'd be stepping into a quagmire.

"Hell with it," she said, pressing the fast forward button on her remote. "I'm not going out with that man."

She took a deep breath and looked out the picture window at the view of the city now sparkling against a field of black. Between adjacent tall buildings, she could see the string of lights outlining the Golden Gate Bridge.

If she lost her job, she'd certainly have to move out of this apartment with its privileged views. But that wouldn't be the end of the world.

With the mental toughness that'd ensured her rapid ascent in a male-dominated career, she refused to think about Albert any longer. Instead, she swept away the debris of her dinner, took a hot bath, set her alarm, and curled up with a steamy romance novel. In her fantasies, a real relationship with a good man was well within the realm of possibility.

Miranda Jones pushed more Cadmium Yellow Medium Hue paint from the tube onto her pallette. To it, she added a touch of Hansa Yellow, then experimented by using her brush to swipe through a touch of Naples, just to see whether the mixture would give her the variation of depth she wanted.

She loved the Daniel Smith paint: the luminous, vivid transparency, how easy they were to work with, and how permanent the hues. She also liked that she could get the same array of colors, whether she worked in watercolor, or in oils, as she did today.

She glanced around the Bays Arts Co-op Studio and Gallery where she was one of several artists who rented space. More than a cubicle, less than a closed room, each of them had three standing walls on which to hang completed pieces, plus work tables, easels, small display tables, and bins for posters and prints.

Two slots away from the large plate glass window in front, Miranda's heard some comings and goings, but paid no attention, lost in her work.

This April, she found herself craving the color yellow. Every touch of it drew her eye, whether of a forsythia bush in bloom, a school bus trundling by, or a bright canary umbrella on someone's balcony.

By training and by inclination, she usually painted from life: from seeing something, seeing *into* it, or studying its surface, or sometimes even seeing *through* it to notice the layer behind, and how that context affected her understanding of the subject. Sunset on clouds, distant hills, tiny grasses less than a foot away, the eyelashes on a big cat, the muscled stance of a buck silhouetted on a ridge. All of it mattered, informed her consciousness, and spoke to her heart.

There were others days that she painted from an inner vision—a close-up detail she hadn't realized she'd noticed, or an "inscape" that began to take form. Today was one of those days. She'd become aware of this morning, as though puzzle pieces began to assemble. By this afternoon, she knew she'd have no choice but to access the developing image by the most direct route—picking up her paint brush. It'd felt electric today, when brain-met-hand-met-brush-met-paint-met-paintboard.

And most of it was coming out yellow. Well, I suppose spring itself is pouring through me out onto the paper. Then, suddenly, it seemed complete. The upper portion of the image was bright, solid blue; the middle, a band of sapphire; the front, a high wall of hundreds of tiny blossoms in bloom, each its own shade of yellow, and all of them iterations of mustard.

It's gotta be in bloom all over the hills south of here. I just have to go see them for myself.

Cast of Characters

Samantha Hugo: early 50s, 5'9, cognac-brown eyes, redhead, statuesque, sharp dresser; Director of Milford-Haven's Environmental Planning Commission; Miranda's friend; Jack Sawyer's former wife; a journal writer.

Meredith Jones: early 30s, 5'8, teal eyes, medium-length brunet hair, beautiful, shapely, athletic; San Francisco financial advisor; Miranda's sister.

Miranda Jones: early 30s, 5'9, green eyes, long brunet hair, beautiful, lean, athletic; fine artist specializing in watercolors, acrylics and murals; a staunch environmentalist whose paintings often depict endangered species; has escaped her wealthy Bay-Area family to create a new life in Milford-Haven.

Zelda McIntyre: early-50s, 5'1, violet eyes, wavy black hair, voluptuous, dramatic and striking; owner of private firm Artist Representations in Santa Barbara; Miranda's artist's rep; corporate art buyer; has designs on Joseph Calvin.

Sally O'Mally: early 40s, 5'3, blue eyes, blond curly hair, perfectly proportioned; owner of Sally's Restaurant; owner of Burn-It-Off; born and reared in Arkansas; Miranda's friend; dislikes Samantha; secretly involved with Jack Sawyer.

Kevin Ransom: late-20s, 6'8, hazel eyes, sandy hair, strong jaw-line, lean, muscular without effort; Foreman at Sawyer Construction; innocent, naive, kind; tuned in to animals; technologically adept; highly intuitive; has longings for Susan Winslow.

Cornelius Smith: early 40s, 6'3, indigo-blue eyes, black hair, handsome, lean; grew up in Milford-Haven where his parents still live; a professional astronomer who works part time at NASA Ames and plans to build an observatory in Milford-Haven; a loner, an eccentric.

COLOPHON

The print version of this book is set in the Cambria font, released in 2004 by Microsoft as a formal, solid font to be equally readable in print and on screens. It was designed by Jelle Bosma, Steve Matteson, and Robin Nicholas.

The name Cambria is the classical name for Wales, the Latin form of the Welsh name for Wales, *Cymru*. The etymology of *Cymru* is *combrog*, meaning "compatriot."

The California town of Cambria is named for its resemblance to the south-western coast of Wales, where the town of Milford Haven has existed since before ancient Roman times, and is mentioned in William Shakespeare's *Cymbeline*.

The dingbat is the Angel Wing Shell, drawn by artist Mary Helsaple, and rendered graphically by cover designer Kevin Meyer. The mussel is a bivalve marine creature that lives on exposed shores in the intertidal zones in California, Florida, the U.K., and Japan, and on other beaches throughout the world. The shells, which are longer than they are wide, often with dark blue exteriors and silvery interiors, when open, resemble a pair of wings.

LIGHTHOUSE

Each of the *Milford-Haven Novelettes* features a real lighthouse. In this holiday story in the Milford-Haven saga, the featured lighthouse is in Florida, and is included because of the red "Christmas" color of its top lens housing that sits atop its black-and-white striped tower.

The St. Augustine Light Station, though private, is still an active aid to navigation in St. Augustine, Florida. It stands at the north end of Anastasia Island and its building was completed in 1874.

This is the second lighthouse in this location, but St. Augustine was the site of Florida's first lighthouse, built by the American Territorial Government on the site of an earlier watchtower built by the Spanish in the late 16th century. The region has a rich history of conquest and exploration, making it a critical location for navigational assistance. The lighthouse swayed severely in the Charleston earthquake of 1866, figured in the Civil War, and was used during World War II as a training station and lookout for enemy ships and submarines.

In 1980, fifteen members of the Junior League of St. Augustine signed a 99-year lease and began a massive restoration project for the grounds that included working with the Coast Guard to restore the tower itself. Despite damage, the original first-order Fresnel Lens was also restored, the first such undertaking in the country.

Today, the St. Augustine Lighthouse and Maritime Museum includes the 165-foot tower, the Keeper's House, as well as other buildings, open to the public. It is also a National oceanic and Atmospheric Administration weather station.

https://www.visitstaugustine.com/thing-to-do/
st-augustine-lighthouse-and-museum

Secret of the Shells

*Special Messages about a Woman and Her Self,
and about Discovering the Next Chapter . . . of Her Life*

Shell - Angel Wing: *When Angels Paint*

- Each book in the series features a special shell icon. This shell belongs to a marine gastropod, whose two sides, when opened, resemble angel wings. Their shape and pure white color refer to the angel references in this book. Have you ever collected shells? Do you use them for decoration?

- How important is intuition? Do you tend to dismiss your "funny feelings"? Or do you always follow them?

- What exactly is an angel? An actual being? A mythological character? Have you ever experienced protection from something you might call an "angel"?

- How do you deal with danger? Do you consider yourself well prepared for disasters? Would you reach out for help from a stranger? Would you respond if a stranger asked for your help?How important is artistic expression in your life? Is it a valued outlet to get rid of stress? Do you enjoy crafts? Do you consider "talent" to be a rare and genuine thing? Do you have artistic talent? Can anyone paint?

- How do you feel about artists? Do you think they should get a "real job" and not expect others to give them grants or special privilege? Do you think an artist should give him/herself a deadline on making a living? Should they have a fall back position in case they don't?

To discover more about the Secrets of the Shells
visit www.MaraPurl.com.
To reach the author, by e-mail: MaraPurl@MaraPurl.com.
by mail: Mara Purl c/o Milford-Haven Enterprises
PO Box 7304-629
North Hollywood, CA 91603

When Angels Paint

Reading Group Topics for Discussion

1. The novellas and novelettes in this series stand alone, while the novels are written in more of a serial format. Do you enjoy holiday stories? What are some of your most—or least—favorite things about the holiday season?

2. In this novelette, we get our first glimpse of Christmas in Milford-Haven, California, where there's no winter weather in the traditional sense. Did you get a sense of the holiday spirit in a small, coastal town?

3. The story focuses on artist Miranda Jones, who moved to Milford-Haven a few months earlier but already enjoys some special friend-ships and traditions. So you believe someone can move away from a vibrant city like San Francisco and feel at home in a small town?

4. What does a professional painter's career include? Does she just paint when she feels inspired? Or does she also take work for hire? How much does an artist need to study in order to have the skills to create work that pleases others and sells?

5. Miranda uses several different media in her work, including large murals and the miniature paintings featured in this book. She paints with oils, acrylics, and watercolors. Does she have a favorite? Does a particular style of painting appeal to you more than others?

6. In addition to being a novelist, Mara Purl is also a former journalist who has interviewed artists and researched their careers. For her novel series, she consults with two artists to get details correct. Do you find her depiction of Miranda's career to be realistic?

7. Why is this book called When Angels Paint? Do you believe Miranda received guidance? Was it spiritual? Was it intuitive?

To share or print these discussion points please visit:
http://marapurl.com/books/what-the-soul-suspects

Find yourself in . . .

Milford-Haven

Small town simplicities . . .
Global complexities . . .

"Where Jack, Zack, Miranda, Cornelius, Samantha, Rune, Meredith, Connie, Emily, Kevin, Joseph, Sally, Tony, Zelda, Notes, Susan, and Cynthia, are building, buying, painting, observing, planning, rehearsing, advising, traveling, reporting, cogitating, dominating, dishing, dealing, conniving, playing, sneaking, and seducing, respectively."

Subscribe to the Milford-Haven Podcast!
Enjoy the original BBC radio drama
with an all-star cast,
original music & sound effects,
plus Bonus Material!

Also available on CD or in downloadable formats
www.MilfordHaven.com

 **Mara Purl,** author of the best-selling and critically acclaimed Milford-Haven Novels, Novellas & Novelettes, pioneered small-town fiction for women.

Mara's beloved fictitious town has been delighting audiences since 1992, when it first appeared as *Milford-Haven, U.S.A.*©—the first American radio drama ever licensed and broadcast by the BBC. The show reached an audience of 4.5 million listeners in the U.K. In the U.S., it was the 1994 Finalist for the New York Festivals World's Best Radio Programs.

Mara was named the Top Female Author for Fiction by *The Authors Show,* and to date, her books have won more than sixty book awards, including the American Fiction, Benjamin Franklin, National Indie Excellence, USA Book News Best Books, and ForeWord Books of the Year.

The Milford-Haven Novels, set in the late 1990s, capture the spirit of adventure and the soul of small-town life, interweaving the tales of three multi-generational women who find romance, friendship and success on California's gorgeous Central Coast.

Mara's other writing credits include plays, screenplays, scripts for *Guiding Light,* cover stories for *Rolling Stone,* staff writing with the *Financial Times* (of London), and the *Associated Press.* She is the co-author (with Erin Gray) of *Act Right: A Manual for the On-Camera Actor.*

As an actress, Mara was "Darla Cook" on *Days Of Our Lives.* For the one-woman show *Mary Shelley: In Her Own Words*—which Mara performs and co-wrote (with Sydney Swire)—she earned a Peak Award. She has co-starred in multiple productions of *Sea Marks* and plays the title role in *Becoming Julia Morgan.* She was named one of twelve Women of the Year by the Los Angeles County Commission for Women.

Mara is married to Dr. Larry Norfleet and lives in Los Angeles and in Colorado Springs.

Visit her website at *www.MaraPurl.com* where you can subscribe to her newsletter and link to her social media sites.

She welcomes email at *MaraPurl@MaraPurl.com.*

MARA PURL
Milford-Haven

Find Saga Chronology at MaraPurl.com/Books